Sniff

by
Lynne Hudson

WINDMILL
BOOKS

Hello, my name is Scruffy,
and I've lost my blanket.

4

Where can it be?
It's snuggly and warm
and smells just like me.

I know, I'll sniff it out!

So I lift up my nose to sniff the air.

Sniff! Sniff! Sniff!

What's that smell on the ground – over there?

A gross, sweaty sock. YUCK!

That stinks!

But it's better ahead.

I think I'll follow this nice smell instead.

The smell is so tempting –
rich, buttery, and sweet.
My tummy is rumbling ...

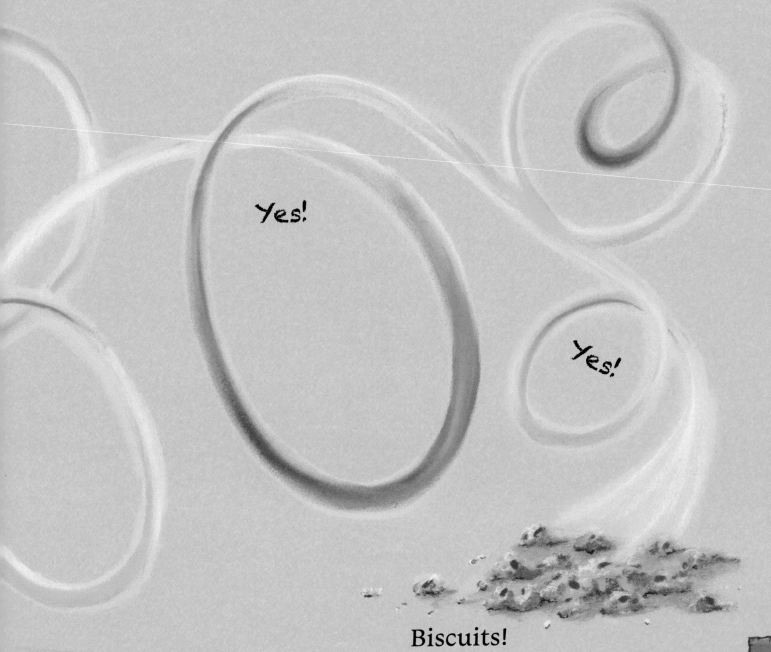

Sniff! Sniff! Sniff!

... is it something to eat?

Yes!

Yes!

Biscuits!

They tasted good, but I still haven't found my blanket.

Sniff! Sniff! Sniff!

I find more smells as I follow my nose –
the damp, mossy ground,
a bluebell and rose,
the smell of a rabbit
and a prickly hedgehog ...

... but they're not my blanket,
and they don't smell of dog.

So I sniff and I snuffle
as I scurry around
'til I smell something new –
look what I've found!

Sniff! Sniff! Sniff!

There on a line
flapping high, all alone,
is a big checkered blanket,
which reminds me of home.

It's clean and it's fresh
and it's billowing and bright.
It looks like my blanket,
but ...

17

Sniff! Sniff! Sniff!

... it doesn't smell right.
So I'll grab it and pull it
and tug 'til it's free.

19

Then I'll rub and I'll roll ...

... 'til it smells just like me!

For Elloura and Lorelai

Published in 2022 by Windmill Books,
an Imprint of Rosen Publishing
29 East 21st Street, New York, NY 10010

First Published in Great Britain in 2016 by Hogs Back Books Ltd.
Text copyright © 2016 Lynne Hudson
Illustrations copyright © 2016 Lynne Hudson

Written by:
Lynne Hudson

Illustrated by:
Lynne Hudson

Cataloging-in-Publication Data

Names: Hudson, Lynne.
Title: Sniff / Lynne Hudson.
Description: New York : Windmill, 2022.
Identifiers: ISBN 9781499489774 (pbk.) | ISBN 9781499489798
(library bound) | ISBN 9781499489781 (6pack) | ISBN 9781499489804
(ebook)
Subjects: LCSH: Dogs--Juvenile fiction.
Classification: LCC PZ7.H837 Sn 2022 | DDC [F]--dc23

Printed in the United States of America

CPSIA Compliance Information: Batch CWWM22: For Further
Information contact Rosen Publishing, New York, New York
at 1-800-237-9932

Find us on